Hello Kitty®
Ice-Skating Fun

by Maria S. Barbo
Illustrated by Sachiho Hino

SCHOLASTIC INC.

ISBN 978-0-545-50209-2

© 1976, 2012 SANRIO CO., LTD. Used Under License.
All rights reserved. Published by Scholastic Inc.,
557 Broadway, New York, NY 10012. Scholastic and assorted logos are trademarks and/or registered trademarks of Scholastic Inc.
12 11 10 9 8 7 6 5 4 3 2 1   12 13 14 15 16 17/0

Printed in the U.S.A.   40
This edition first printing, November 2012
Designed by Angela Jun

The big day was finally here!
Hello Kitty and her friends were going to
ice-skate together.

Hello Kitty loved to skate.
She wore her favorite skating outfit.
She had on her fuzzy pink sweater.

She even placed a bright shiny crown on her head.

Hello Kitty could not wait one more minute. Papa gave her her mittens and pretty purple scarf.

She made sure her skates were tied tightly.
She was ready to go!

Hello Kitty saw Tracy skating fast.
Whoosh! He skidded to a stop.
Uh-oh! Tracy sent ice flying all over
Hello Kitty's pink sweater.

Tracy was sorry.
Hello Kitty laughed.
Maybe Tracy could teach her how to
skate fast.

Hello Kitty skated slowly onto the ice.
There were so many skaters today!
Then Hello Kitty saw someone jumping and
spinning on the ice.
It was Joey!
Hello Kitty waved to him.

Could Joey teach her how to skate?
Hello Kitty thought it would be fun to learn
how to skate fast and twirl.

Tracy showed Hello Kitty how to skate fast.
Joey taught her how to twirl and spin.
Skating was hard work, but fun!

This was the best day of ice-skating
ever!
But someone was missing.
Fifi! Why was she late?

There was Fifi!

She was all dressed up.

She wore a special dress made just for skating.

She even had brand-new ice skates.
Fifi looked pretty.
She was happy to see her friends.

Fifi took a step onto the ice.
But her new skates were not tied!
Uh-oh!

Fifi slipped and fell.
Then she spun around and around.

Fifi was not hurt.
But her dress was wet.
Her hat was crushed.

Her new skates were dirty.
Oh, no!
Fifi started to cry.

Hello Kitty knew her friend was a little
bit scared.
Hello Kitty loved to skate.
But skating wouldn't be as much fun
without Fifi.

Hello Kitty had an idea!
She called to Tracy and Joey.
They had a job to do.
They had to get Fifi back onto the ice.

Joey showed Fifi his super-high jump.
Tracy showed her how fast he could
skate.

Hello Kitty showed Fifi the new twirl she had learned.

Then Hello Kitty skated over to Fifi.
Hello Kitty gave Fifi her bright shiny
crown to help her feel brave.

Fifi smiled.
Her eyes brightened.
Hello Kitty was a good friend.
Fifi gave Hello Kitty a hug.

Surprise! Papa brought them all
hot cocoa. He put extra marshmallows in
Fifi's cocoa.
Then it started to snow.
Yay! What a great day!

They couldn't skate without Fifi.
Would she try again?
Fifi nodded.

This time Fifi made sure her skates
were tied tightly.
Then Fifi slowly stepped onto the ice.
The four friends held hands.

They skated in a line.

Good job!
Everyone was a great skater.
Fifi laughed.

Then Tracy and Joey raced around
the rink.

Hello Kitty showed Fifi how to spin and twirl.

Ice-skating was fun.
But Hello Kitty knew that skating with all
of her friends was the most fun of all.